FIVE REASONS WHY WE LOVE THIS BOOK:

IT'S AN **ELECTRIFYING** STORY

There's double trouble, as Creature makes a friend who's almost as naughty as he is!

The illustrations are **SHOCKINGLY** brilliant.

You will laugh until your hair stands on end!

PAAARRRP!

A sneaky peek of what's inside!

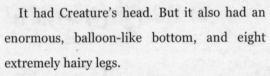

It had Creature's head. But it also had an enormous, balloon-like bottom, and eight extremely hairy legs.

'He's turned into a *spider*!' Nora gasped.

Alexis opened her eyes a crack, screamed, and closed them again. Jake felt the hairs on the back of his neck rise. Then he remembered the new Creature.

'Where'd the other one go?'

They all looked round. The new Creature was nowhere to be seen.

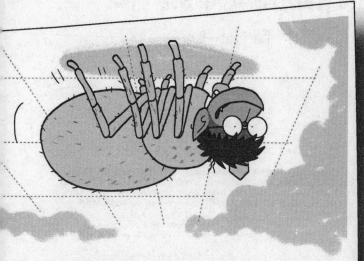

Nora bit her lip. 'What shall we do?'

Jake looked up at Spider-Creature on the ceiling. 'We'll have to try to catch Creature first, then look for the new one . . . oh no, where's he going now?'

Spider-Creature was skittering along the ceiling. Jake and Nora ran after him, followed reluctantly by Alexis.

'Why do you think he keeps changing?' Jake called to Nora as they dodged tables, trying to keep Creature in their sights.

Fo Dad, a scientist at heart —S.W.

For Paul—D.O'C.

OXFORD
UNIVERSITY PRESS

Great Clarendon Street, Oxford OX2 6DP

Oxford University Press is a department of the University of Oxford.
It furthers the University's objective of excellence in research, scholarship,
and education by publishing worldwide. Oxford is a registered trade mark of
Oxford University Press in the UK and in certain other countries

British Library Cataloguing in Publication Data available

Data available

ISBN: 978-0-19-274441-8 (paperback)
ISBN: 978-0-19-274442-5 (eBook)

2 4 6 8 10 9 7 5 3 1

Printed in Great Britain

Paper used in the production of this book is a natural,
recyclable product made from wood grown in sustainable forests.
The manufacturing process conforms to the environmental
regulations of the country of origin.

CREATURE TEACHER
SCIENCE SHOCKER

SAM WATKINS and
ILLUSTRATED BY David O'Connell

OXFORD
UNIVERSITY PRESS

CHAPTER 1:

HAVE YOU GOT A TISSUE?

'Hi! Welcome to the Whizz-BANG Science Fair!'

A girl in a T-shirt with a lightning bolt on it shoved a leaflet into Jake's hand.

'Err . . . thanks,' he mumbled, as she disappeared into the crowd.

Jake stuffed the leaflet into his pocket, took a deep breath and began to push his way across the lobby of the Natural History Museum. He was late—he should have been here an hour ago to help set up the Class 5b exhibit. Now it was ten o'clock, the fair had opened, and the museum lobby was jam-packed with excited people, all jostling to get into the main hall.

Something whacked his elbow.

'Excuse me—Goliath bird-eating spider coming through!'

'Sorry...' Jake backed away as a boy squeezed past, carrying a large glass tank. Inside, he saw a brown, hairy spider the size of a small rat.

'You can stroke her if you want,' the boy said. 'She doesn't bite ... normally ...'

Jake was saved by a shout.

'JAKE—over here!'

His friend Nora was standing by the doorway

to the main hall. With her were two more of his classmates, Karl and Barnaby. He wriggled through the sea of bodies to them.

'Where've you been?' Nora grumbled. 'It's only two hours till the judging.'

'Sorry. Connie decided to play hide-and-seek as we were leaving.'

Nora rolled her eyes. 'Haven't you told your sister how important this competition is?'

'I tried, but she stuck her potty on her head,' Jake said.

Barnaby's eyes widened and he nudged Jake. 'Talking of potty . . .'

Jake turned to see the tall, bespectacled figure of their teacher, Mr Hyde, bobbing through the crowd. He was wearing a white lab coat, khaki shorts, purple socks, and sandals.

Karl chuckled.

Nora frowned. 'Don't be mean about Mr Hyde.'

Jake nodded, although Barnaby did sort of have a point. Mr Hyde didn't look exactly normal. But then, Mr Hyde wasn't *normal*—he

was *extraordinary*. Officially the Best Teacher in the Universe. But he did have one teeny, tiny, humungous problem . . .

'We'll have to keep an eye on Mr Hyde today,' Jake muttered to his friends. 'Imagine the chaos if he turned into Creature in here.'

Nora nodded, then put her finger to her lips as Mr Hyde bounced up.

'There you are, Class 5b whizz-kids!' he cried. 'Are you ready for the Whizz-BANG Brainiest Whizzkid Competition? We can win, you know—I've got a nose for these things! Come along. Alexis and Woodstock are waiting . . .'

As Mr Hyde hustled the pupils into the main hall, Jake was surrounded by a dizzying cocktail of bangs, flashes, and stinks. Everywhere, tables were piled high with chemical concoctions and electronic gizmos. In the centre of the hall, a gigantic volcano belched out sulphurous fumes every few seconds.

Mr Hyde marched off, with Jake and his friends scurrying along behind. As they rounded the volcano, Jake stopped.

Mrs Blunt, their Headteacher, was standing a few metres away.

Jake felt a pang of guilt, even though he'd done nothing wrong. Mrs Blunt had that effect on you. She was standing guard over a large object covered in a sheet.

'Class 5a's exhibit,' Nora whispered.

'What is it?' Jake asked in a low voice. 'They've kept it really quiet.'

'Whatever it is, it's not working,' Nora said. 'Amelia was yelling some *very* rude things at it earlier.'

Everyone giggled. Amelia Trotter-Hogg, also known as Most Annoying Person in the

Universe, was always trying to cause trouble for them, but Mrs Blunt thought she was a package of pony-tailed perfection.

Mrs Blunt's guilt-inducing aura had no effect on Mr Hyde.

'Morning, Mrs Blunt!' he sang, breezing past the scowling Headteacher. Jake shuffled past, looking at the floor. He could feel her laser eyes boring holes in his skull.

'Oh, look,' he heard Nora say. 'Someone's taken the stand next to ours. It was empty earlier.'

Jake peered at the sign. '"ANT ANTICS". Hey, Nora, you like bugs . . . Nora?'

Nora had shot behind him, a look of horror on her face.

'Keep walking,' she muttered, head down,

clinging to his arm. Jake looked over as they passed the Ant Antics stand, curious to see what had freaked Nora out. A frizzy-haired boy with glasses was standing at a table, talking loudly to a group of children.

'Hurry!' Nora hissed, chivvying Jake towards their stand. In front of them, Mr Hyde stopped and clapped his hands, beaming.

'There she blows!'

Jake grinned. Their exhibit was pretty cool.

Officially it was called 'Have You Got a Tissue?' At least that's what Nora called it. Everyone else called it the Giant Nose. Or just 'The Nose'.

The Nose was mainly Nora's idea. It was built from papier-mâché and was the size of a kid's playhouse. When you pulled a lever on the side, a bucket-load of purple snot sneezed out of the nostrils. Nora liked the fact that it demonstrated the workings of the human immune system. Everyone else just liked the fact it was a giant nose.

Woodstock and Alexis were putting some finishing touches to the Nose as Nora shot past and stood fuming with outrage next to it.

'Whoa!' exclaimed Woodstock, nearly dropping his paint.

Jake peeked round. 'What's up, Nora?'

'The boy on the Ant Antics stand!' Nora said through gritted teeth. 'It's that dreadful know-it-all, Isaac Einstein. He thinks he knows everything there is to know about bugs. How ridiculous is that?'

'Totally ridiculous,' Jake agreed.

'Imagine if he wins . . .' Nora groaned.

'He won't, because *we're* going to win,' Alexis declared. 'Our exhibit is educational and fun. Isn't it, Nora?'

'I like your thinking, Alexis!' Mr Hyde's head popped round the Nose. 'WHAT ARE WE, FOLKS?'

'Winners,' mumbled everyone.

'Louder!' cried Mr Hyde.

'WINNERS!' they all shouted.

'BEEEEEEEEEEEEEEEE-E-E-E-E-E-P!'

A foghorn-like beep rattled Jake's eardrums. Something cold and metallic gripped his arm and swivelled him round.

Jake blinked twice. 'What on earth?!'

CHAPTER 2:

RULE BOT

A robot was standing in front of Jake. The front of its head was a screen, on which was displayed a very grumpy face. A flashing blue police siren sat on its head.

Before Jake could move, a sticker popped out of a slot in the robot's tummy. The robot shot a metal arm out, grabbed the sticker and slapped it on Jake's forehead.

13

'A Sad Face!' exclaimed Karl.

'What?!' Jake peeled the sticker off. It was, indeed, one of Mrs Blunt's Sad Face stickers. Sad Face stickers were given to pupils who broke the school rules. If you got three Sad Faces you had to work on Mrs Blunt's Rockery, shifting humungously heavy rocks.

'VIOLATION OF RULE 63— NO SHOUTING!' the robot barked, sounding suspiciously like an electronic Mrs Blunt.

'It must be 5a's project!' Nora cried. 'They got it working!'

Woodstock groaned. 'So that's what the old dragon's been hiding—HEY!'

The robot had planted a sticker on his chest.

'VIOLATION OF RULE 27—NEVER CALL THE HEADTEACHER AN OLD DRAGON,' the robot rasped.

Barnaby snorted, and got a sticker for violation of Rule 41—No Snorting.

Mr Hyde scratched his head.

'Well, it's very impressive, if a tad overenthusiastic,' he said. 'I'd never have thought Class 5a would be so good at robotics. Listen up, guys, I'm going to grab a coffee. I'll be back in a jiffy.' He strode off.

'NEWT! I thought I saw you go past!' came a loud, nasal voice.

Nora ducked, but too late. The frizzy-haired

boy from the Ant Antics stand was peering round the Nose.

'My name is *Nora*,' Nora growled.

'Oh yes. Sorry—I never remember first names.' Isaac squinted at the Nose through his thick glasses. 'So, what exactly is this?'

'It's a nose,' Nora said darkly.

'Ah.' Isaac walked round the Nose. He pointed to the lever. 'What's that?'

'That is what is known as a lever.'

'I know, but what does it *do*?'

Nora put a bucket under the nostrils. 'Pull it.'

'Aaaaaaaaaa-CHOO!'

Two waterfalls of lurid purple snot exploded out of the nostrils into the bucket.

Isaac dipped his finger in.

'Purple. I hypothesize . . . potassium permanganate?'

Nora looked smug. 'Wrong. It's sugar, flour, and water. And purple food dye.'

'I hate to say this, Newt—snot is green, not purple. All to do with the neutrophils. What happens is—'

Nora crossed her arms. 'You don't have to explain, Isaac. I know everything about noses. As for the colour, well, Woodstock was in charge of the snot, and he wanted purple.'

'It's more . . . artistic,' Woodstock mumbled, looking guiltily at Nora.

Isaac was bending down to peer up a nostril when Alexis hissed.

'Look out, here comes trouble . . .'

'Now THAT is the DUMBEST thing I've ever seen.'

Jake groaned. Amelia Trotter-Hogg, Most Annoying Person in the Universe, was standing smirking at him. Behind her hovered her two only slightly less annoying friends.

'What *is* that thing?' Amelia asked. 'Wait—I know. It's a Load of Rubbish.'

This was obviously the funniest joke ever, judging by the screeches of laughter from Amelia's friends.

Amelia looked at Barnaby's Sad Face sticker and sniggered.

'I see Rule-Bot got *you* already, McCrumb.'

Barnaby pulled the sticker off, crossly.

'Rule-Bot? Is that its name? Pain-in-the-Bot, more like . . .'

Amelia shrugged. 'Say what you want. *We're* going to win the competition. You won't be so rude then, because we'll be on the Rise and Shine TV Show . . . and Mrs Blunt says we'll be famous, and—'

'Mrs *Blunt* said that?!' Nora exploded. 'Is that all she cares about—being famous?! The best part of the prize is a day at Space

Cadet School. That's way better than being on TV!'

'Huh, you *would* think that . . .'

'Hello, what's going on?' Mr Hyde had reappeared. He stepped between Amelia and Nora. 'It's good to be competitive, but can we do it in a friendly way?'

Amelia scowled.

'Fine. Good luck, Class 5b,' she said. 'You're going to need it,' she then mouthed at Jake so Mr Hyde couldn't hear.

'That's more like it,' Mr Hyde said. 'Can we return the gesture, 5b?'

There was a tense silence. With an effort, Nora spoke.

'Amelia, your robot is . . . interesting. Do tell me how you made it.'

Amelia looked shifty. 'Oh, bits of computers—that sort of thing . . .'

'How does it talk?' Karl asked.

Amelia shrugged. 'I dunno. I didn't do that bit.'

Jake leaned forward. 'Who did do that bit?'

'That was the Profess—'

'Shhhh!' one of her friends hissed. Amelia put her hand over her mouth.

'Profess . . . Professor?' said Jake, slowly. 'Hang on . . .'

Amelia's eyes darted around like a cornered warthog. She started to back away, talking at top speed.

'What does it matter, cos we're going to win and be on telly and we'll be celebrities and rich and . . . oh, I've had enough of this. Come on, Rule-Bot, let's leave the Class 5b bores to their stupid snot machine,' she snapped. Her two friends reattached themselves to her sides and they stalked off, followed by a whirring Rule-Bot.

Jake's cheeks felt hot. He turned to the others.

'Did you hear that bit about a professor?'

Woodstock looked grim. 'They got someone to make their robot.'

'That's against the rules!' Alexis exclaimed. 'The pupils have to make the exhibits themselves. Don't they, sir?'

'Well, yes,' Mr Hyde said. 'But we don't have any proof—let's not jump to conclusions . . .'

'They cheated,' Karl said.

'They used a professor,' Nora said.

'An EVIL professor, I bet,' Woodstock added, his fringe quivering.

'Right, that's enough,' Mr Hyde declared, looking more and more uncomfortable. 'I'll look into it. Perhaps we should check out some of the other competitors, eh? See what we're up against. I vote we pop next door to Isaac's stand. I'm dying to see what antics these ants are up to!'

CHAPTER 3:

MAKE SPARKS FLY

Alexis, Karl, and Barnaby decided to stay at the Nose while the rest of them trailed off to see Isaac's exhibit.

Jake's mind raced. Class 5a had *clearly* cheated—Mrs Blunt was so desperate to be famous she'd do anything to win! *But Mr Hyde's right—we don't have any proof...*

'Now *that's* what I call science!' Isaac's voice

interrupted his thoughts.

The Ant Antics table was in front of them. On it sat a huge glass tank, filled with earth. As Jake looked closer he saw a maze of tunnels running through the soil, with black specks scuttling along them.

'This is our formicarium,' declared Isaac. 'It contains approximately ten thousand ants.' He poked Nora. 'Newt, remember last year when I beat you by one question in the quiz because you didn't know what a formicarium was?'

'I didn't know that, either,' said Mr Hyde quickly, as Nora's glasses began to steam up. 'Interesting display. Fascinati . . .'

His voice trailed away.

'Hello! So many keen young scientists here today!'

A woman with glasses and a bubbling mass of red, curly hair had popped up behind the formicarium. Jake couldn't help noticing that she had planets dangling from her ears.

Nora stared at her. 'Ooh, I love your earrings. Saturn's my favourite planet.'

The woman's eyes twinkled. 'Mine too!' She turned to Mr Hyde. 'I'm Miss Jex, Isaac's teacher. And you are . . .?'

Mr Hyde's mouth opened, then shut.

'Mr Hyde,' Woodstock said, helpfully.

'Lovely to meet you! What's your exhibit?' Miss Jex looked at Mr Hyde again.

He made a strangled noise. 'Haaa ... haaaaaa ... Have You Got a Tissue!'

'Bless you!' Miss Jex said. 'It is a bit fumy in here!' She fished in her pocket and handed him a tissue. Mr Hyde looked at it blankly.

'Kip ... per?'

Kipper?! With a jolt, Jake realized that his teacher had turned a shocking shade of pink. Mr Hyde was changing! *He's got himself in a tizzy because he thinks Isaac's exhibit is loads better than ours! We have to get him away ...*

He nudged Nora, who was still staring at Miss Jex. 'Look, her eyes are different colours,' she whispered. 'One's blue and one's green, they're amazing!'

'Stop looking at Miss Jex and look at Mr Hyde—he's changing!' Jake whispered back. Louder, he said, 'We should go back to our stand, sir . . .'

'Ooh—can I come?' Miss Jex asked.

Jake bit his lip. *We have to get Mr Hyde on his own!*

'Shouldn't you stay here, to, um . . . feed your ants?' he said. 'They look hungry . . .'

'Isaac can look after the ants, can't you dear? Come on—I'm dying to see your stand!'

Miss Jex began pulling Mr Hyde away, chattering non-stop.

'. . . can't wait for the judging . . . SO excited about Space Cadet School!' Jake, Nora, and

Woodstock trailed along behind, throwing each other anxious looks. 'And the space shuttle trip sounds FANTASTIC, doesn't it?'

Mr Hyde found his voice. 'What . . . what space shuttle trip?'

'The space shuttle simulator at Space Cadet School,' said Miss Jex. 'You get to go into orbit and see the Earth from 250 kilometres above the surface!'

Mr Hyde's face went from shocking pink to ghastly green.

'I'm afraid that sounds a tad terrifying to me,' he mumbled. 'I'm hopeless with heights.'

'What a shame!' Miss Jex patted his arm. 'Well, I hear they've got these amazing zero gravity toilets . . . OOH!'

Miss Jex pointed excitedly to a table not

far from their stand. A sign on it read 'MAKE SPARKS FLY!' On the table, Jake saw a large metal globe on a pole. A girl was fiddling with it.

'A Van de Graaff generator! When you touch the globe the static electricity makes your hair stand on end. Come on . . .'

She pulled Mr Hyde across to the table.

'Can we have a go?' Miss Jex asked.

'It's not working,' the girl said. 'I've changed the wires, but nothing's happening.'

Cautiously, Miss Jex placed her hand on the globe. Nothing happened. She peered at the wires. 'Positive, negative—hmm. It seems OK.'

Mr Hyde coughed and straightened his tie.

'Let me see, Miss Jex,' he said in an oddly deep voice. 'I know about these things . . .'

Mr Hyde leaned over, putting his hand out to steady himself on the table.

His hand missed. He fell forwards, grabbing the metal globe as he did so.

CRRRRRRRRRRRAAAAAACK!!!!!

A sizzling shower of sparks flew out of the globe!

Both teachers' hair stood on end like two deranged dandelion clocks. Mr Hyde's eyes crossed and Miss Jex's earrings spun round and round.

Bzzzzzzzzzzzzzzzzzzzzz‾z‾z‾z‾z . . .

'TURN IT OFF!' yelled Woodstock.

The girl behind the table clicked a switch frantically. 'I can't!'

'Pull their hands away!' shouted Nora.

Jake felt a shock run up his arm as he

grabbed Mr Hyde's hand and yanked it off the globe. Nora did the same with Miss Jex.

Bzzz . . . zzz . . . ZWUP.

A crackle. Then silence.

Phew, Jake thought, rubbing his arm. He looked around. A crowd had gathered, all staring curiously at the two teachers' frizzed-up hair.

Miss Jex took her glasses off.

'That shock must have done something to my eyes,' she said, blinking. 'Mr Hyde—you look positively luminous!'

'Uh-oh,' Woodstock murmured.

Jake sucked in a breath.

His teacher was bathed in a shimmering orange glow. A strong smell of burning rubber wafted into Jake's nostrils . . .

He's changing into Creature, Jake realized.

'BACK TO THE NOSE!' He grabbed one of Mr Hyde's arms. Nora grabbed the other.

'Make way! Electric-shock victim coming through!' Woodstock shouted.

The crowd parted as they pulled Mr Hyde to their stand, skidded up to the Nose, and shoved the glowing teacher behind it . . .

BANG! An eye-meltingly bright flash of light.

FAAAAAAAAAAAAAARRRRRT!

Wheeeeeeee . . . .

POP! POP! POP!

BANG!

CHAPTER 4:

FUN WITH FROGSPAWN

For a few seconds, Jake couldn't see anything through the billowing cloud of purple smoke. Then he began to make out a shadowy figure through the haze.

'Mr Hyde?' he called. 'I mean—Creature? Is that you?'

'No, it's me.' Woodstock emerged from the smoke, coughing.

As the smoke cleared, two more shadowy figures turned into Nora and Barnaby. Creature was nowhere to be seen.

Alexis and Karl emerged from the smoke.

'What happened? Did something explode?' Alexis asked.

'Mr Hyde's turned into Creature,' Jake sighed.

Karl groaned. 'Oh, man . . . where is he?'

'I don't know,' Jake said. 'But we have to catch him.' He paused as he stared around him. 'Hey, what's happening?'

A crowd of excited people had gathered in front of the Nose, pointing and chattering excitedly.

'What was that bang?'

'Cool—an exploding nose!'

'Can you make it explode again?'

'Errr . . .' Jake and his friends looked at each other, confused by the barrage of questions.

'LET ME THROUGH! Newt! What's going on?'

A red-faced Isaac stomped towards them.

'What was that explosion?!' he squawked. 'I was giving a fascinating presentation on the digestive systems of arthropods when my whole audience disappeared!'

'Oh. Well, sorry about that,' mumbled Jake, trying to sidestep round him. Isaac blocked his path.

'And where on earth is Miss Jex?' he demanded. 'The judging is starting soon—she really should be at the stand!'

Behind Jake, Nora inhaled sharply. 'The

judging is starting soon? What are we going to do?'

'Don't worry about the judging now,' Jake whispered, beckoning his friends over. 'We've got to find Creature . . .'

'So what are we waiting for?' Alexis whispered. 'Let's go!'

'What are you whispering about?' Isaac asked, poking Nora on the arm. 'And where *is* Miss Jex?'

'I don't know, Isaac,' Nora said. 'She was here a minute ago! Maybe she went to get a coffee? Teachers love coffee. Now leave us alone.'

Isaac tromped off, muttering under his breath.

'Finally!' Jake said, relieved. 'Right. We need two people on the stand to deal with all these people. The rest of us will look for Creature.'

'I'll stay,' Karl offered. 'I'm good at crowd control.'

'I'll stay too,' Woodstock said.

'OK,' Jake said. 'Nora, Alexis, let's go.'

'How about me?' Barnaby asked.

'You can't come,' Nora said.

Barnaby glared. 'Why not?'

'Because you're a troublemaker.'

'Am not.'

'Yes you are!'

Jake ground his teeth. 'We don't have time for this! Okay Barnaby, you can come with us if you promise not to cause trouble.'

He paused. In the corner of his eye he caught a flash of blue light. The unmistakable shape of Rule-Bot was gliding towards them through the crowd. *How could they look for Creature with Rule-Bot hovering around?*

Jake had a sudden brainwave.

'On second thoughts,' he said to Barnaby. 'Start causing trouble!'

Barnaby stared. 'What?'

'Rule-Bot's coming this way. Lure him away!'

'How?' Barnaby was confused.

'Just do what you're good at! He'll follow you, and leave us free to find Creature.'

Barnaby's eyes gleamed. 'Cool!'

He ducked under the table and sauntered towards the approaching Rule-Bot. He stopped just in front of the robot and said something that Jake couldn't hear.

'BEEEEEEEEEP!!!!'

Rule-Bot's screen face went from slightly sad to flaming furious in a matter of milliseconds! Jake saw one, two, no, *three* Sad Face stickers shoot out of his tummy slot.

Barnaby wasn't about to get stickered again. He leapfrogged over the robot and shot off across the hall, whooping.

Rule-Bot spun around three times and gave chase, its siren wailing and light flashing like a fruit machine that was about to pay out.

'I wonder what Barnaby said?' Alexis grinned.

Jake shrugged. 'It worked, anyway. Come on.'

He started to push through the crowd of students swarming around their stand.

Explosions were firing off on loads of stands, and clouds of evil-smelling, coloured smoke were filling the room. A loud bang from a nearby stand made him jump.

'Our explosion was better than yours!' shouted a boy on the stand, seeing Jake looking.

Jake frowned. 'I think we've started some sort of explosions competition,' he muttered to Alexis and Nora, dodging out of the way of a harassed-looking museum worker who was charging across the hall, yelling at everyone to stop blowing things up.

'At least no one will see Creature in this smoke,' Alexis spluttered, as another putrid cloud wafted over them.

'Yeah, but neither will we.' Jake waved the smoke away.

Nora grabbed him. 'Over there—under the table!' She pointed.

Jake peered through the haze. Just ahead, a teacher was arranging large glass jars on a table. Underneath the table, Jake spotted the

unmistakeable furry shape of Creature with his shock of black hair on his head, and a large pair of glasses perched on his nose. He was holding something up to his mouth. Jake, Nora and Alexis crouched down to get a better look.

'What's he got?' Jake whispered, creeping closer.

'Looks like a jar of clear jelly,' Nora said.

At that moment, the teacher placed a cardboard sign on the front of the table.

Jake looked at the sign:

FUN WITH
FROGSPAWN

They all looked at each other. 'That's not jelly,' said Alexis.

'It's FROGSPAWN!!' squeaked Nora.

'Stop him!' Jake cried.

All three of them made a dash for the table.

Creature opened his mouth wide and tipped the slimy contents of the jar into it.

CHAPTER 5:

CLONING ABOUT

Jake, Alexis, and Nora froze, as Creature swallowed the frogspawn in one gulp. A look of enormous surprise came over his face.

'**HIC!**' Creature shot into the air.

THUNK. His head whacked the underside of the table, making all the jars jump. The teacher on the stand stared at them.

'Funny! The frogspawn is lively today,' he

said. But then a loud explosion on the next stand sent him diving for cover.

Jake crept forward. 'Now's our chance . . .'

He stopped.

What was happening to Creature? His back legs were getting longer . . . and skinnier . . . and greener . . . till they looked like . . . *frog's legs?*

'R-r-r-ribbit?' Creature croaked, taking an experimental hop. 'R-r-r-ribbit!'

'He's turned into a frog!' Alexis squeaked.

Nora shook her head. 'Only his bottom half! He's half-frog, half-Creature. The electric shock must have done something to his molecules—'

BANG!

The biggest explosion yet ripped through the hall, followed by a mushroom cloud of noxious green smoke. With a croak, Creature rocketed out from under the table and took a wild leap on his froggy back legs, straight over Jake's head.

'After him!' Alexis cried.

Jake and his friends chased after Creature.

Most people seemed to making a headlong dash for the main entrance to escape the smoke, but Creature didn't seem bothered by it. He hopped the other way, and disappeared into the smoke cloud. Taking a deep breath, Jake plunged in after him. Smoke filled his eyes, making them water. *Where'd he go?* Aha—just ahead—a glimpse of a bright green bottom . . .

'This way,' Jake shouted to Nora and Alexis, who were stumbling along behind him. He emerged, spluttering, from the fog, to see Creature hop up onto a table covered in plants. There was no one on the stand—everyone had made a dash for the doors.

A sign on the table read 'PLANT POWER', and a pot of yellow marigolds stood in the centre.

Creature stared at the marigolds, mesmerized. Jake, Nora, and Alexis tiptoed closer, waiting for their chance to pounce.

Closer . . . closer . . . From here, Jake could see why Creature was fixated on the flowers. A shiny green fly was buzzing round them.

Creature's back legs tensed, ready to spring on the fly. Jake froze, ready to spring on Creature . . .

'Kippuuurrrrr?'

Jake saw Creature stagger back in surprise and almost fall off the table. A furry, bespectacled face was rising up on the other side of the flowerpot.

Jake gasped.

Another Creature was gazing at Creature through the marigolds!

Jake stared at the new Creature. It cocked its head to one side. Creature cocked his head at the same time. It cocked its head the other way. Creature did too. It was almost as though they were looking at themselves in a mirror—even down to the glasses!

The only thing that was different about them was the hair. Creature had a shock of black hair on his head. The new Creature had a bush of red hair.

'Has Creature been cloned, do you think?' Nora whispered. 'I saw an exhibit called "Cloning About" earlier.'

'But the hair's different,' Jake said. 'Aren't clones supposed to be identical?'

Nora shrugged. 'Yes normally—but maybe they haven't quite perfected their cloning technique.'

Creature suddenly leaned forward, picked a marigold, and held it out to the new Creature.

'Eeeee?' The new Creature looked at the flower . . . just as the green fly decided, rather foolishly, to land on it.

KER-SNAP! In less than a millisecond, a long, green froggy tongue shot out of Creature's mouth, curled round the unlucky fly, and hoiked it back into his mouth. It was so quick, the new Creature didn't even seem to see it happen. It reached out its hand for the flower.

Creature opened his mouth and his tongue flopped back out again, the fly still stuck to the end, buzzing angrily.

Creature picked up his tongue, pulled the fly off, and offered it to his new friend.

'KIP-PUUURRRRR!!'

The new Creature batted the fly away crossly. Suddenly it spotted something interesting over Creature's shoulder. It jumped down from the table and scampered away across the smoky hall. Creature nearly tripped over his still-hanging-out tongue as he hurtled off in pursuit, clutching his flower. Nora, Jake, and Alexis raced after them.

'They're going to wreck the place!' Jake cried, as they tried to keep up with the two Creatures, who were leapfrogging over every table in their way, knocking chemistry experiments flying. Nora was just behind him.

'I know—but how can we catch two? One's bad enough—WATCH OUT!!'

Jake skidded to a halt, narrowly avoiding a gush of steaming liquid from an experiment through which the two Creatures had just steamrollered.

He wiped his forehead. *That was close!*

'Now's our chance,' Alexis said, pointing.

Ahead, Jake saw Creature catch up with the new Creature and offer it the now rather battered marigold. Jake started to run forward, but Nora grabbed him.

'Awwwww, wait, Jake. That's so sweet.'

The new Creature looked at the marigold. Then it stuffed it in its mouth, chewed, and swallowed.

'BUUUURRRRRPPP!'

Then it picked its nose, and hoiked out a large, green bogey. It shyly offered the bogey to Creature.

Creature squeaked happily. He reached out and took the bogey, flattened it out and carefully stuck it to his chest, like a badge.

'Ugh!' Nora said, making a face. 'Not so sweet!'

The new Creature poked Creature playfully, jumped to its feet, and scuttled off into the smoke cloud, heading towards the huge volcano in the centre of the hall. Creature bounded after it, with Jake, Nora, and Alexis on his heels. Jake saw that Creature's froggy legs had disappeared and he was back to his normal, furry self.

As they rounded the volcano, Alexis stopped, and her face went a sickly shade of frog green.

'Oh no! I don't like the look of this at ALL.'

CHAPTER 6:

SPIDERS AREN'T SCARY

'What is it?'

Jake peered round the volcano, trying to see what had spooked Alexis.

A few metres away, the two Creatures were crouching in front of a table stacked with glass tanks.

A sign read: 'SPIDERS AREN'T SCARY'.

'Fab—spiders!' Nora said, stepping forward.

Alexis yanked her back.

'No *way* am I going near those things!'

'You shouldn't be scared of spiders, Alexis,' Nora said, crossly.

'I'm not scared.' Alexis took a deep breath. 'I'm . . . um . . . allergic to spiders.'

Jake recognized the biggest tank. Inside it he could just see the monster spider he'd

narrowly avoided stroking in the lobby earlier.

Nora peered at it. 'Looks like a tarantula.'

'It's a Goliath bird-eating spider,' Jake said.

Alexis groaned and closed her eyes.

Nora looked impressed. 'How—' She stopped, her eyes widening. 'Ohhhhh, no!'

'What's happening?!' Alexis squeaked.

Creature had jumped up next to the tank, squashed his face to the glass, and was making faces at the huge, hairy spider. The spider glared back at him through eight glittering, black eyes.

Creature cackled. He glanced down at the new Creature, as if to say, 'Aren't I funny?!'

The new Creature squawked crossly, as if to say, 'No, you are not.'

Jake shook his head. 'He'll make it angry.

We've got to stop him.'

'You grab him, I'll grab the new Creature,' Nora said, grimly.

'Eeeeek!' The new Creature suddenly gave a shrill squeak. Creature was pulling the lid of the tank off! He put a paw in and fished the spider out of the tank.

'STOP!' Jake dashed forward.

Creature spun round, the spider crouching on his paw.

'Eeeeeeeee?' Creature said. He held the spider up to his lips . . .

'DON'T EAT IT!' shrieked Nora.

. . . And gave it a big kiss.

The spider gave Creature a withering look with all eight eyes.

Then it bit him on the nose.

'Kip-PEEEEERRRRRRRRR!!!'

Creature dropped the spider back into tank and rocketed upwards, vanishing into the cloud of smoke that still lingered around the ceiling.

Jake ran forward, arms outstretched to catch him . . .

But Creature didn't fall back down. Confused, Jake peered up. *Where was he?* Then, through a gap in the smoke, he saw a brown, hairy shape on the ceiling.

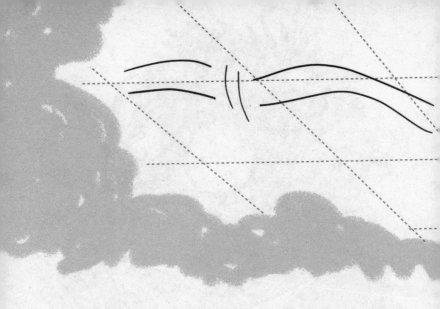

It had Creature's head. But it also had an enormous, balloon-like bottom, and eight extremely hairy legs.

'He's turned into a *spider*!' Nora gasped.

Alexis opened her eyes a crack, screamed, and closed them again. Jake felt the hairs on the back of his neck rise. Then he remembered the new Creature.

'Where'd the other one go?'

They all looked round. The new Creature was nowhere to be seen.

Nora bit her lip. 'What shall we do?'

Jake looked up at Spider-Creature on the ceiling. 'We'll have to try to catch Creature first, then look for the new one . . . oh no, where's he going now?'

Spider-Creature was skittering along the ceiling. Jake and Nora ran after him, followed reluctantly by Alexis.

'Why do you think he keeps changing?' Jake called to Nora as they dodged tables, trying to keep Creature in their sights.

'Well, it's just a guess, but maybe the electric shock jumbled his cells up, so now he can change into anything, given the right catalyst.'

'What's a catalyst?' Jake asked.

'A chemical that sets off a reaction, like a trigger—'

'GET DOWN!' Alexis suddenly hissed.

Jake looked round. 'What?'

'Rule-Bot!'

Class 5a's robot was rolling towards them. Jake, Nora, and Alexis dived behind a stand. *Had he seen them?* Jake peered out, cautiously. Rule-Bot had stopped in front of the 'Make Sparks Fly!' stand.

Nora tutted. 'Barnaby's supposed to be keeping Rule-Bot busy! Where's he gone?'

'*Everyone's* gone,' said Alexis.

Jake looked round. Now the smoke was clearing, he could see that the hall was nearly empty of people. At the far wall, a museum worker was wafting smoke out of a window.

'They'll be back once the smoke's cleared,' Jake said. 'Then there'll be trouble.'

'Squarrrk!'

A startled squawk came from above. Jake looked up.

Creature's bulbous spider bottom was shrinking, and his fur was changing back to red-brown. One by one, his spider legs were disappearing. As they did so, Creature was coming unstuck from the ceiling!

Jake held his breath. *He's turning back into normal Creature—and I'm too far away to catch him!*

Creature was now hanging on with one last spider leg. As it changed back into a normal paw, it lost its grip on the ceiling, and Creature fell into space.

'Nooooooo!' Nora cried, clutching Jake's arm so hard he squeaked.

But Creature clearly still had a bit of spider in him. No sooner had he fallen than a strand of silver thread fired out of his bottom like a grappling hook. It hit the ceiling and stuck fast. Creature began to float gently down on his silver rope.

Jake breathed out. 'Phew . . . OW!' Nora had clutched his arm again.

'You know where he's going to land, don't you?'

Jake's eyes widened. 'On Rule-Bot's head!'

Rule-Bot was still in front of the
Make Sparks Fly stand, staring
at the Van de Graaff generator.
A large, flashing love heart
appeared on his screen.

He beeped softly.

Jake, Nora, and Alexis stared,
open-mouthed, as Creature floated

down . . .

down . . .

down . . .

till he was hanging just over the unsuspecting Rule-Bot's head.

Creature blew a loud raspberry.

The love heart on Rule-Bot's screen vanished, to be replaced with a very sad face. His head whizzed round. But although his head could swivel in a full circle, he couldn't look up. So he couldn't see Creature at all.

Creature blew another, louder raspberry.

Rule-Bot spun round so fast he nearly fell over. Alexis giggled, but Jake ran forward.

'Hey, Rule-Bot! Over here!' he shouted at the confused robot.

Too late.

SNAP! The silver thread broke.

Creature dropped—CLUNK!—onto Rule-Bot's head.

CHAPTER 7:

ANT ANTICS

For two seconds, nothing happened.

Then everything happened. All at once. Very fast.

'BEEEEEEEPPP!!!' Rule-Bot's head whizzed round and round, his blue light flashing madly.

'Wheeeeeeeeeeeee!' Creature clung on for dear life, legs flying out behind him. On the third spin, he lost his grip, catapulted through the air and landed on the Make Sparks Fly table, just missing the Van de Graaff generator.

Rule-Bot charged after him, his claw-like hand outstretched . . .

Creature stepped to one side.

CLANG! Rule-Bot's metal hand slammed into the Van de Graaff generator.

CRAAAAAAAAAACK!!!

A burst of blue sparks exploded from Rule-Bot's head.

'VIOLATION OF RULE SEVEN THOUSAND THREE HUNDRED AND TWO—NEVER JUMP ON RULE-BOT'S HEAD!' the robot rasped.

Nora stared. 'There's no such rule!'

Rule-Bot turned to face Nora. 'VIOLATION OF RULE EIGHT MILLION AND SEVENTY THREE—DO NOT CONTRADICT RULE-BOT!'

Jake, Nora, and Alexis dived out of the way as a stream of stickers flew out of Rule-Bot's tummy slot. People were filing back into the hall now, and a crowd started to gather around the sparking, spinning robot.

'STAND BACK! Let me deal with this . . .'

A red-faced Mrs Blunt was bulldozing her way through the crowd. She pointed a remote control at Rule-Bot.

CRACKLE . . . SIZZLE . . . WHOOSH!!

A shower of multicoloured sparks exploded from Rule-Bot's head.

'VIOLATION OF RULE TWO BILLION AND ONE! MADAM, YOU ARE UNDER ARREST!' shouted Rule-Bot at Mrs Blunt.

'You can't arrest me, you dim-witted droid,' Mrs Blunt snapped. She crouched down and pointed the remote at Rule-Bot's tummy slot.

'Mmmmmmmffff!'

A stream of stickers flew out, covering the Headteacher's face. She let out a muffled shriek and tried to peel them off, but they just kept on coming until she could barely be seen under a thick layer of Sad Faces. A few people rushed forward to try and help, but they just got stickered themselves. It was an extremely stickery situation.

'Kipperrrrrrrrrrrr . . .'

Jake dragged his eyes away from the chaos to see Creature perching on the end of the Make Sparks Fly table, gazing across at the Ant Antics stand.

Jake tensed, and inched forwards.

Slowly . . . don't scare him . . .

Jake sprang . . .

. . . but his elbows hit the table where Creature had been a second before. As he scrambled up, he saw Creature bouncing towards the Ant Antics stand.

'After him!' Jake shouted to Nora and Alexis. Leaving the sticker battle behind, they pushed through the crowd after Creature . . . Jake saw Creature reach the stand and hop up onto the edge of the formicarium, where he perched, swaying, and peered around.

I bet he's looking for that new Creature, Jake guessed. He looked around too, but couldn't see it anywhere. Luckily, neither Isaac nor Miss Jex were anywhere to be seen, either.

'GOTCHA!'

Alexis hurled herself past Jake, towards Creature. Alarmed, Creature turned, wobbled, then tumbled into the formicarium in an explosion of dirt and ants.

Jake, Nora, and Alexis ran forward to try to grab him. But as they closed in, he leapt back up and began dancing around like a loon, slapping himself all over.

'The ants are biting him!' Nora exclaimed.

Biting? Alarm bells jangled in Jake's head as he remembered Nora's earlier words:

Creature can change into anything given the right catalyst.

'STAY BACK!' he cried.

He pulled Alexis and Nora backwards—just as two antennae burst out of Creature's head, his eyes went all buggy and a pair of humungous mandibles sprouted from his chin.

CLICK! CLACK! Ant-Creature snapped his new, shiny mandibles.

At the same time, Jake heard a familiar electronic rasp.

'ANT INVASION DETECTED! ANTI-ANT PROGRAM ACTIVATED! EX-TERM-IN-ATE! EX-TERM-IN-ATE!'

Rule-Bot!

Creature's buggy eyes nearly popped out as Rule-Bot charged towards the table at top speed. Jake ran forward to stop him, but Rule-Bot turned at the last minute—too sharply! He spun out of control, straight into one of the table legs.

CRACK!

The leg snapped. Nora gave a cry.

'The table!' she shouted. 'It's going over!'

They all dived forward and grabbed the edge of the table as it started to teeter . . . but the huge formicarium was too heavy.

'Can't . . . hold . . . it,' Jake panted, as the formicarium, ten thousand ants, and one Creature slid with a horrible grinding noise towards the edge . . .

C-R-A-SHHHH!!!

The tank smashed into a thousand tiny pieces on the floor.

The three pupils gaped in appalled silence.

Nora put her hands to her mouth. 'Isaac will go mad!'

A carpet of angry ants began to spread out from the wreckage. Creature sat, dazed, in the middle of it as Rule-Bot wheeled round to face him, siren wailing.

'EX-TERM-IN-ATE!

EX-TERM-IN-ATE!'

Jake tried to dart in front of the robot, but had to jump back to avoid a blast of blue sparks.

'HEY! What's going on?!'

Karl skidded up, Woodstock and Barnaby behind him.

'Rule-Bot's trying to exterminate Creature,' Jake shouted. 'We've got to stop him!'

The six pupils fanned out around Rule-Bot, now covered in ants. He screeched to a halt, trying to sweep them off with his mechanical hand.

'ALL ANTS ARE UNDER ARREST!'

The ants kept crawling. Rule-Bot got crosser and crosser. He swivelled his head towards Creature.

'BAD KING ANT. MAKE SMALL ANTS ATTACK RULE-BOT. EX-TERM-IN-ATE!'

'I can see the off-switch!' shouted Nora, suddenly. 'Distract him!'

Alexis, Karl, and Woodstock dashed in, yelling and waving. But Rule-Bot kept rolling towards Creature, metal arms outstretched menacingly. Jake could see that Creature's antennae and mandibles were shrinking—he was changing back into normal Creature, and he looked completely terrified.

'It's not working!' Nora cried. 'Barnaby— you try!'

Barnaby ran to one side and started blowing raspberries.

'You're nothing but a tatty old toaster!' he shouted.

Jake got the idea.

'Work together, everyone! Over here, you worn-out wheelie bin!' he yelled.

'Lazy lawnmower!'

'Horrid Hoover!'

Rule-Bot's head swung round to face the yelling pupils. As soon as his head was turned, Nora took her chance. She dived under his arm.

'Got it!' She pushed a button.

There was a crackle, and a hum.

'*Bedtime,*' Rule-Bot said in a sad, tinny voice.

His screen flickered, and went black.

CHAPTER 8:

LAVA PALAVER

Everyone ran to the quivering Creature. Jake looked round, anxiously. Had anyone seen what had happened? But people were only just starting to come back into the hall, and most of them were busy trying to clear up the mess caused by all the explosions earlier.

'He's covered in ants!' exclaimed Alexis, crouching down and brushing ants off

Creature's nose.

'Poor thing! Are you okay?' Nora asked.

Creature stared at her, and squeaked softly. Then he closed his eyes. Jake heard a faint humming.

'Hmmmmmmmmmmmm . . .'

Woodstock nudged Jake. 'Look!'

Jake stared. A faint, wobbly heat haze surrounded Creature. There was a loud rumble.

'Kipperrrrrrr?' Creature looked at his tummy quizzically.

'He's changing back into Mr Hyde! We have to get him back to our stand,' said Nora.

She whisked Creature up and stuffed him under her lab coat. Jake and others formed a protective huddle around her as they hurried back to the Nose.

A series of violent rumbles made the floor vibrate under their feet.

'Where can we put him?' Nora cried.

Jake looked round. 'In the Nose!'

They pushed Creature inside, and stood back. Jake covered his eyes, waiting for the fireworks. The rumbling got louder and louder. Jake waited expectantly for the usual signs of the change—bright lights . . . fart . . . pop! pop! pop!

But something was different. The rumbling didn't seem to be coming from Creature! So where was it coming from? Jake took his hands away from his eyes.

The hall was packed with people again. But all the people were standing as still as statues, all facing the same way, all staring at . . .

The volcano exhibit! Jake grabbed Nora.

'It's not *Creature* that's rumbling!' he shouted. 'It's the volcano!'

All six pupils wheeled round. As they did so,

the volcano let out a piercing squeal.

Wheeeeeeeeeeeeeeeeeee . . . .

'I think something's stuck inside it,' Nora exclaimed.

WHEEEEEEEEEEEEEEEEEEEE . . .

The squeal got louder and louder. Everyone in the room covered their ears . . .

 POP!

With a sound like the biggest ever champagne cork popping, a large, oddly-shaped lump of rock shot out of the top of the volcano, trailing a sticky red lava trail behind it. It whizzed across the hall, right over Jake's head. As it sailed over, he heard it making a very un-rocklike noise.

'KIPPPPPPPPPPPURRRRRRRRRRRRRRRR!!!!!'

it shrieked, arm stretched out in front of it like Superman. Unlike Superman, it landed with a painful-looking thump, and rolled through a door at the back of the hall.

Nora was beside Jake like a shot.

'That was the new Creature!' she cried.

'What new Creature?' a familiar voice said behind them.

Jake turned. 'MR HYDE!'

Mr Hyde was standing where the Nose had been. He was covered in the mangled remains of the Nose and had purple snot dripping down

his face, but apart
from that he looked normal.

Jake had been so busy watching the
volcano erupt that he hadn't even noticed
Creature changing back into Mr Hyde!

Mr Hyde looked down at himself.

'Why am I wearing a papier mache dress?'

'It's the Nose, sir. We hid you in it when you
started changing,' Jake said. 'I forgot you'd get
bigger when you changed back.'

Everyone ran to help free their teacher. As
he stepped out of the last few tattered remains
of the Nose, Mr Hyde looked at Nora.

'What was that you were saying about a new Creature?'

'Yes, what did you mean, Nora?' Karl chimed in. Barnaby and Woodstock leaned forward, eyes wide.

'Well . . . there was another Creature that looked just like you,' Nora explained.

'But it disappeared when you changed into a spider.' Jake added.

'A spider?' Woodstock interrupted. 'Mr Hyde turned into a spider?!'

'Yes—that was after he changed into a frog . . .'

'A frog?' Karl looked disbelieving.

'It's true! And before he turned into—'

'An ant.' Mr Hyde finished his sentence.

Jake blinked. 'You remember?'

'I remember bits,' Mr Hyde said, slowly. 'Like you remember a dream. I remember eating a jar of weird-tasting jelly . . . and then wanting to hop around. And I remember the spider biting me on the nose, and next thing I was running around on the ceiling . . .'

'I didn't like it when you were a spider.' Alexis said.

'I quite enjoyed it,' said Mr Hyde. 'I didn't like being an ant, though. That shouty robot scared me. But I remember you lot protecting me, and that gave me a warm, nice feeling . . .'

'Don't you remember the new Creature?' Nora asked.

Mr Hyde shook his head. 'Not at all. Are you sure? How on earth could there be another Creature?'

'We think—' Nora took a deep breath. 'In fact, we're pretty sure—you have been cloned.'

Mr Hyde stared. 'Cloned?'

Jake explained. 'One of the exhibits is a cloning experiment. We think you must have somehow got into it, and cloned yourself.'

'Only it didn't quite work,' Nora added. 'The new Creature has different hair to you . . . '

Karl's eyes widened. 'Oh man. Clone Creature. Double trouble!'

Barnaby's eyes went misty. 'Wish *I* had a clone!'

'I don't know,' Mr Hyde said. 'I think I'd remember being cloned . . .'

'But you don't remember the new Creature, either,' Jake broke in. 'That's definitely real— *and* it's running around somehow in the next hall,' he reminded Nora. 'We have to go and find it!'

Mr Hyde suddenly shot bolt upright.

'Yes, we should—RIGHT NOW!'

Jake looked at his teacher's panic-stricken face. 'What's the matter, sir?' he asked.

Mr Hyde gulped.

'If it is a clone of Creature—will it change back into a clone of ME?'

Jake's mouth fell open. But before he could say anything, there was a shout.

'HEY! Nora Newton! I need to talk to you!!'

A wild-eyed Isaac was streaking across the hall towards them.

CHAPTER 9:

A BIT OF AN
EYE-OPENER

Nora gulped. 'Isaac! He must have seen the formicarium . . .'

Isaac skidded to a halt in front of them.

'What's the matter, Isaac?' Mr Hyde asked.

'I have to show you something,' he whispered, glancing round furtively. Jake threw Nora an anxious glance. Mr Hyde's brow creased.

'It's a bit difficult—'

'Oh please, you must!' Isaac begged.

Mr Hyde relented. 'Weeeell . . . OK. But we'll have to be quick.'

Isaac nodded. 'Follow me!'

Jake thought Isaac would take them to his stand. But instead, he led them to the back of the hall and out through the same door the new Creature had disappeared through. They emerged into another hall, full of telescopes and astronomical globes.

'Keep your eyes peeled,' Jake whispered to the others. 'The new Creature came this way!'

'Over here,' Isaac called. He was standing in front of a door with a sign on it that read 'EMERGENCY USE ONLY'.

Mr Hyde frowned. 'Isaac, I don't think—'

'This *is* an emergency,' Isaac said. 'You'll

understand in a minute.'

He pushed the door open and stepped inside.

'Oh dear . . .' Mr Hyde hesitated, then followed Isaac. Jake and the others crowded in behind them.

It took a moment for Jake's eyes to adjust to the dark. Monstrous pale shapes draped in white sheets loomed in the gloom. *A storeroom*, Jake thought.

'We shouldn't be in here,' Mr Hyde said. His voice boomed back.

'HERE . . . here . . . here. . .'

Barnaby burped. 'BURP . . . burp . . . burp . . .'

'Shhhh!' Isaac said. 'You'll scare it.'

'Scare what?' Karl asked.

Isaac walked across the nearest sheet, and carefully lifted the corner.

'Look,' he whispered.

Jake peered underneath—then jolted back! He was looking straight into the tooth-lined jaws of a monster! Then he realized what it was.

'It's just a dinosaur skull,' he said. But wait—
what was that? Two pinpricks of light. *Eyes!*
Little, bright eyes, moving towards him . . .
a brown, furry shape . . .

'Kippurrrrr?' it said.

Jake stared, speechless. *The new Creature!*
It hopped up onto the dinosaur's lower jawbone
and peered inquisitively at Isaac.

'It's . . .' Nora's voice trailed off.

Isaac looked at her. 'Do you know something
about this?'

Nora gulped. Mr Hyde spoke. 'Nora, let me
explain. That Creature is . . . well, it's ME.'

'What?!' Isaac spluttered.

'It's true,' Mr Hyde said. 'I change into a
Creature just like this.'

Everyone started talking at once.

'And today, while he was Creature—'

'—he somehow got cloned!'

'And now there are two—'

'Stop—listen . . .' Isaac shook his head. The new Creature shook its head too. As it did so, something jingled in its hair. Nora pointed.

'Look! Miss Jex's earrings!'

Dangling from each of the Creature's ears Jake saw the Saturn-shaped earrings Miss Jex had been wearing earlier.

Barnaby grinned. 'It must have stolen them!'

Nora rolled her eyes. 'She'll go mad!'

'LET ME SPEAK!!!' Isaac shouted.

Everyone stopped talking.

'The Creature isn't Mr Hyde,' Isaac said. 'And it didn't steal Miss Jex's earrings.'

Nora looked puzzled. 'So who . . .'

Isaac cleared his throat. 'The Creature IS Miss Jex!'

There was an astonished silence.

'*Miss Jex?!!*' Mr Hyde's mouth fell open.

Isaac nodded. 'I couldn't find Miss Jex earlier, so I went back to our stand. I found this Creature hiding under Miss Jex's coat.

I thought it had escaped from another stand. It ran off and I lost it in all the smoke and chaos. I went round the whole museum looking for Miss Jex. As I was coming back through the astronomy hall I saw the Creature run into this storeroom, so I followed it. When I finally caught it, I realized that it *was* Miss Jex!'

'How do you know for sure?' Mr Hyde asked, looking pained.

'The red hair and glasses were the first clue. And the earrings almost convinced me. But I'm a scientist—I need proof. Glasses and earrings don't *prove* anything . . .' Isaac picked up the wide-eyed little Creature. 'But EYES do.'

Jake stared at the Creature. It stared back. There was something odd about its eyes . . . then he twigged what it was. One was sapphire blue, the other emerald green!

Nora gasped. 'Miss Jex has different-coloured eyes'

Isaac turned to Nora. 'I thought I was going mad! Then I thought of you, Nora. Thought you might have an idea about how this happened.'

Nora stared. 'Me?! But I thought you thought my ideas were *silly!*'

Isaac looked surprised. 'I don't think that,' he said. 'You're clever—the cleverest person I know.'

Nora flushed. 'Oh, um, thanks,' she mumbled, embarrassed.

A door banged on the other side of the storeroom, making everyone jump.

'Someone's coming,' Woodstock hissed.

'Time to go! Here . . .' Mr Hyde grabbed

Miss Jex from Isaac, stuffed her under his coat and ran to the door. 'Hurry!'

One by one they ran through, back into the astronomy hall.

Mr Hyde looked around. 'We have to get Miss Jex out of the museum.'

'The only way is back through the Science Fair,' Isaac said.

They trooped back into the main hall, that now looked more like a major disaster zone than a Science Fair. But as they approached the door to the main entrance, Jake saw Mrs Blunt standing right in front of it, a grim look on her face.

'Bad idea. Back to the stand,' Mr Hyde said, turning on his heel. As they approached the Ant Antics stand, Jake saw a group of smartly dressed people standing in front of it. His mouth suddenly felt like he'd eaten dry crackers. *Is it the Museum Police? Are they looking for Miss Jex? Will they arrest us?*

A loudspeaker crackled.

'Would the "Ant Antics" and the "Have You

Got a Tissue" teams please return to your stands immediately, to present your work to the judges.'

CHAPTER 10:

TEN THOUSAND ANTS AND A BUCKET-LOAD OF SNOT

'The judges!' Isaac gulped. 'I'd totally forgotten about the competition!'

One judge spotted them.

'Are you the Ant Antics team?' she called, waving a clipboard.

'We've been waiting for you,' said another, staring at them over steel-rimmed spectacles.

'For approximately fifty-three seconds,' said

another, rapping his watch.

Isaac shuffled forward. 'It's just m-m-e,' he stammered. 'My teacher has, um, well, changed . . .'

'Gone to *get* changed,' Mr Hyde said quickly, pulling his coat round the bulge that was Miss Jex. 'She got lava all over her from the volcano.'

Jake saw that even the judges looked a bit lava-splattered. The judge with the clipboard, who seemed to be the head judge, frowned.

'Most unfortunate, but I'm afraid we can't wait. Please proceed.'

Isaac cleared his throat.

'Ahem. Ant Antics is a fascinating project about . . . ants. Um . . . we have approximately ten thousand ants—'

'I don't see any ants,' a judge interrupted.

'Invisible ants?' said another. 'Now that would be a first!'

The judges roared with laughter. The small crowd of onlookers who had gathered to watch the judging laughed too.

Isaac went beetroot red.

'They're not invisible—they're in the formicari . . .'

He pointed. Everyone looked round.

'. . . um . . .' Isaac's voice trailed away. 'It's gone!'

He was pointing at a large, empty, ant-free stand.

Jake gulped. *Isaac doesn't know about Rule-Bot smashing the formicarium!*

He obviously hadn't been back to the stand since it happened. Someone must have been round with a broom—there wasn't a trace of glass or soil anywhere. And not a single ant in sight. Even the broken table had gone.

Should I tell him? Jake decided it wasn't a good moment—Isaac looked like he might burst into tears anyway. Nora ran up to the head judge, who was scribbling 'DISQUALIFIED' on her clipboard.

'Oh, please don't disqualify Isaac! His exhibit was really good—'

'I can only judge what I can see,' the judge snapped. 'Right, moving on. There's still one more exhibit to go.'

Nora went quiet. Jake saw that she was shaking. A vision of the tattered remains of the Nose flashed in front of his eyes. There'd been virtually nothing left after they'd got Mr Hyde out of it! But the judges were already walking towards their stand.

The head judge shuffled her notes. 'The next

one is . . . "Have You Got a Tissue?" Should be—ah, this is it . . .'

There was a stunned silence.

Aargh. I can't look. Jake fixed his eyes firmly on the floor.

As he looked, he saw something moving. *An ant!* It was carrying something. Almost instinctively, he bent down and picked it up. *The last surviving ant. Isaac might want it . . .* He heard an exclamation from Nora. And a cry from Alexis.

'My word,' he heard one of the judges say. 'Extraordinary!'

'Breathtaking!' said another.

'Mind-boggling!' said another.

Jake slowly looked up. He rubbed his eyes, then looked again.

Where the Giant Nose had been there now stood a glistening, purple structure. Nearly as tall as Jake himself, it was covered with a network of delicate, semi-transparent spires and bridges. It reminded Jake of the time his parents had taken him to Disneyland and he'd seen the Cinderella castle at night, all lit up with purple lights.

What on earth was it?! The last he'd seen of their stand, it had been a chaotic mess of purple snot and . . . but wait a minute—

Jake stared at the structure. Something was moving on it. *Ants! Thousands of them . . . what are they doing?* He looked back at the ant that he had picked up.

'Isaac—hold out your hand!' Jake whispered.

Isaac looked surprised but did as Jake asked.

Jake carefully placed the ant on Isaac's palm.

'Look at what it's carrying!' he said. Isaac lifted his hand and stared at the ant. Nora leaned in too. They spoke as one.

'Purple snot!'

'Isaac! Your ants have built a new home with our snot!' she exclaimed.

Isaac blinked. 'Are you thinking what I'm thinking?'

'I think so . . .' She grinned. 'Come on!'

They both ran over to the judges.

'Please . . . Isaac and I would like to introduce our cross-school project,' said Nora.

The head judge flipped through her notes. 'There's nothing here about cross-school projects!'

'Let them speak,' said another judge. 'I think

we should hear what they've got to say.'

'Quiet, please!' called Nora.

Isaac held up the ant that Jake had given him.

'One tiny ant,' he said. 'Can't do much on its own.'

Nora gestured to the ant palace, dramatically. 'But as part of a team, it can create architectural miracles!'

'In order to conduct an experiment into what ants can do when they work together . . .'

'Isaac released ten thousand ants into the wild . . .'

'. . . and using Nora's unique formula of sugar, flour, and water—'

'And purple food dye,' Woodstock called.

'And purple food dye . . . these ants built themselves a new colony . . .'

The judges were enthralled. Jake was too. It was as though Nora and Isaac had rehearsed their whole speech—when he knew they were making it up as they went along!

'So we humans can learn a great deal from ants . . .' Isaac said.

'. . . by working together, we can achieve anything!' Nora finished.

'HURRAY!!!'

A roar of applause made Jake jump. He looked round to find himself surrounded by people, all clapping and cheering. Mr Hyde was wiping his eyes. He saw Jake looking at him, and coughed.

'Bit fumy in here,' he mumbled.

The judges put their heads together, muttering, as the crowd chattered excitedly.

The head judge stepped forward.

'Quiet, please!' she shouted. The hall fell silent. 'The judges will now proceed to the stage to announce the winner of the Whizz-BANG Brainiest Whizzkid Competition.'

CHAPTER 11:

AND THE WINNER IS . . .

The judges marched across the hall. Jake and his friends followed, swept along on a tide of chattering people.

'You were awesome!' Jake said to Nora as they reached the stage.

Nora smiled nervously. 'Awesome enough to win?'

'HA! You've got no chance, goggle girl!'

Jake winced, and turned to see Amelia Trotter-Hogg and her two limpet friends smirking at him.

'And what makes you think you have, Amelia?' Nora snapped. 'Rule-Bot is faulty. He went completely loopy.'

Amelia shrugged. 'We fixed him.'

A flash of anger surged through Jake. 'You mean the *Professor* fixed him?'

'Prove it,' Amelia spat.

'SILENCE, PLEASE!' called the head judge.

Jake could have heard an ant burp in the silence.

'We are pleased to announce . . .'

She paused. Jake's heart leapt.

'. . . that the winning exhibit is . . .'

Oh please . . . it has to be us . . .

'Rule-Bot—the rule-enforcing robot!'

WHAT?! Jake could hardly believe his ears. He couldn't bring himself to look at Nora as Amelia and her friends flounced past them onto the stage, evil glee on their faces.

'MAKE WAY! Winner coming through!'

Mrs Blunt sashayed up the steps onto the stage, where she stood waving regally at the crowd. There was a splatter of polite clapping.

The head judge handed Amelia a microphone. 'Would you like to say a few words?'

Mrs Blunt grabbed the microphone.

'Yes, I would. It is a great honour for me— I mean *us*—to receive this award. The Prof . . . er . . . *pupils* put a lot of hard work into Rule-Bot. Its discipline circuits are second to none— all designed by the pupils, of course . . .'

'VIOLATION OF RULE 999! DO NOT TELL PORKY PIES!' said a tinny voice.

Mrs Blunt glared around. 'Who said that?'

Jake looked round to see a flashing blue light moving jerkily through the crowd. *Rule-Bot!* The robot stopped in front of the stage.

Amelia and her friends shuffled back, uneasily.

'LIE DETECTOR ACTIVATED! PUPILS NOT DESIGN RULE-BOT! PROFESSOR QUARK DESIGN RULE-BOT!'

A murmur rippled round the audience.

'Is this true?' the head judge asked, sternly. 'The rules state that pupils must design their own exhibits!'

'Of course it's not true!' Mrs Blunt smiled through gritted teeth.

'So who is Professor Quark?' said another judge.

'PROFESSOR QUARK DESIGN ROBOTS!' rasped Rule-Bot.

Jake saw a man's face appear on Rule-Bot's screen, with a smile as dazzling as a toothpaste advert.

'Greetings! I am Professor Ignominious Quark. Need a robot? Not got the skills? Better call Quark!' the man oozed, smiling with all his teeth.

'Oooooooooooh!' murmured the crowd.

Mrs Blunt's smile evaporated.

'YOU ARE A CHEAT!' Rule-Bot barked.

'And *you* are a tin-plated traitor!' Mrs Blunt raged, frantically fumbling in her bag. She pulled out her remote control, pointed it at the robot, and stabbed a button.

ZWAP!

Rule-Bot went quiet.

'That's how you deal with a badly-behaved robot!' Mrs Blunt said, triumphantly. 'If only one could do the same for ch—'

Her voice faltered.

Every light on Rule-Bot's metal body lit up.

His head began to spin round, faster and faster, shooting out multicoloured sparks like a Catherine wheel and squealing like a Roman candle.

'SQUEEEEEEEEEEEEEE ...'

'It's going to blow!' someone shouted.

Rule-Bot didn't explode. A sheet of electric blue flame burst from his head and flowed down him like glowing water.

'ALERT! ALERT!' Rule-Bot slurred. 'OVERHEATING! OVEEEEEEERRRRRR ... HEEEEATINGGGGGGGGGGG ... AAAAARGHHHH ...'

With a final tragic sigh, Rule-Bot collapsed in a puddle of molten metal.

Jake stood, stunned, as the crowd surged

forward to gawp at the steaming pool of liquefied robot. The judges looked helplessly out at the chaos.

'Explosions, eruptions, melting robots!' one said. 'What next? The end of the universe?!'

'Look over there, I've never seen Mrs Blunt and Amelia move so fast!' Karl laughed.

Jake looked across the stage to see Mrs Blunt and Amelia scuttling down the steps, looking as though they wanted to melt into the floor too.

'We should stop them,' Alexis exclaimed, ready to spring off after them. 'They can't just get away with cheating.'

Jake grabbed her. 'Leave it. They won't win now, anyway.'

'Who will, though?' Nora said.

Woodstock pointed. 'Looks like we're about to find out.'

The judges were walking to the front of the stage. The head judge clapped her hands.

'Please listen, everyone. This has been a difficult day, to say the least. However, we have chosen a new winner.'

Jake held his breath.

The judge cleared her throat. 'We are happy to announce that the winner of the Whizz-BANG Brainiest Whizzkid Competition is . . . the Ant Palace!'

'HURRAY!!!!' The crowd whooped gleefully.

'Yay!' Jake high-fived Nora. Isaac tried to high-five Jake. He missed and whacked Alexis on the ear instead, but she was too busy gleefully punching Barnaby on the arm to notice.

'Excuse me . . . when you have finished bashing each other, could two of you come up here to collect the medals?' the judge called down to them severely, but Jake thought he saw a twinkle in her eye.

Nora and Isaac bounded onto the stage. The judge hung a gold medal round each of their necks and shook their hands.

'Well done!' she shouted over deafening cheers. Nora and Isaac looked at each other, beaming with pride. Jake thought his face would split from grinning . . . but then he heard a yelp behind him.

'Jake!' Mr Hyde hissed.

Jake turned. 'Sir?'

Mr Hyde's coat was bulging out as if he had a gang of overenthusiastic moles under it. *Miss Jex!* Alarmed, Jake stepped forward . . .

PAAAAAAAAAARP!!!!!

Mr Hyde's coat inflated like a hot air balloon.

Ping! Ping! Ping!

Miss Jex burst out of the coat with a button-busting fart. Jake tried to grab her, but she was too quick for him. With a victorious squawk, she skittered off into the crowd.

CHAPTER 12:

THE FATHER OF EVOLUTION

Jake heard startled shrieks from the crowd as Miss Jex darted between their legs.

'MISS JEX!' cried Mr Hyde, charging after her. Jake, Woodstock, Alexis, and Barnaby tried desperately to keep up.

'Excuse me . . . escaped giant chinchilla . . . perfectly harmless . . . no need to panic . . .'

The crowd panicked.

'WHAT did he say it was?'

'*A gorilla?!*'

'Gorilla on the loose!!'

'CALL THE POLICE!!!!'

As he burst out of the crowd, Jake saw a little brown shape shoot through the door to the museum lobby, with Mr Hyde close behind. As he reached the door, Mr Hyde slammed to a halt and threw himself back against the wall.

Jake caught up. 'What's wrong, sir?' He peered into the lobby.

Mrs Blunt and Amelia were standing at the reception desk, talking angrily to the man behind it. Behind them, Miss Jex was skipping across the floor towards the museum's huge revolving doors.

Jake held his breath. They hadn't seen her . . .

she was going to make it . . .

'KIPPPPPPPPPPPPPPPURRRRRRRRR!!!!'

Miss Jex made an impressive leap into the
revolving doors.

'What the—?' The man at the desk shot up.

'A GIANT RAT!!!' shrieked Amelia, hurling
herself onto the desk.

Mrs Blunt's eyes narrowed. 'Rats don't say "kipper"!' she snarled.

She stalked to the doors. Inside, Miss Jex was running round and round like a deranged hamster in a wheel.

'I've got you now!' shouted Mrs Blunt.

As the doors swung round, she stepped inside and gave them a shove.

Miss Jex catapulted out the other side, landing in the museum's courtyard.

Creeaaaaaaaaaaaaak . . .

Judder judder judder . . .

CLUNK. The doors stopped, with Mrs Blunt inside.

The Headteacher pushed. She pulled. She pounded.

The revolving doors didn't budge. They were broken.

'LET ME OUT!!' she bawled. Soon a crowd had gathered round the stuck doors.

'Everyone keep calm!' the man at the desk hollered. Amelia was still gabbling about giant rats. Jake stepped back, just as Nora and Isaac came running up.

'What's happening?' Nora panted. 'We saw you run off!'

Mr Hyde and Jake hurriedly explained.

'What shall we do, sir?' Karl asked, as people piled past them into the overcrowded lobby.

Mr Hyde frowned. 'Miss Jex could be in danger. We have to go after her.'

'How?' asked Woodstock. 'We can't go out the main door.'

Barnaby pointed. 'Use another door.'

In the corner, almost hidden behind a potted palm, Jake saw a fire exit sign.

'Well spotted,' said Mr Hyde. They ran over. Mr Hyde pushed the bar on the door down and it swung open.

Jake stepped through and found himself in the front courtyard of the museum, next to the steps. A path led to the front gate and a busy road. By the gate Jake saw a statue of a stern-looking man with a flowing beard . . . and a strangely-shaped, furry hat . . .

'Miss Jex is on the statue's head!' Alexis hissed.

'Go slowly—no sudden noises,' whispered Mr Hyde. They tiptoed down the path. Alexis reached the statue first, and started to climb up it. Jake held his breath as she got closer and closer to Miss Jex. She reached out her hand.

'OI, YOU!!'

Everyone froze. A museum worker was running towards them.

'You can't climb on Darwin! He's the Father of Evolution, he is!'

Miss Jex hurled herself off the Father of Evolution and bounced out of the gates. At that moment, Jake saw a moving flash of red through the railings.

'BUS!' he yelled, and took off at a sprint.

Too late! Miss Jex bounced into the road.

SCREEEEEEEEEEEEECH!!

The bus skidded to a standstill as Jake teetered on the kerb. The others ran up beside him. Nora gave a cry.

'Was she hit?'

'I can't see her!'

Woodstock pointed. 'She made it!'

On the other side of the road, a brown furry shape was hopping over a wall.

'Phew!' Mr Hyde wiped his forehead. A loud beep from the bus spurred him into action. He walked into the road and held his hand up.

'Over you go, kids,' he said loudly. Jake shuffled across, trying not to look at the bus driver who was shouting something that didn't sound like 'Have a nice day'. They were barely over when he screeched off with an angry honk. Mr Hyde shook his head.

'Some people! Right, folks—we've got a teacher—I mean, Creature—to catch!'

He vaulted over the wall. Jake and the others followed.

They found themselves in a pretty, tree-lined park, with picnicking families dotted around. It was a peaceful scene.

'EEEEEEEEEEK!!!!!'

Jake saw the people at the closest picnic scatter as Miss Jex bounced onto their picnic rug, picked up a large cake, and guzzled it in one chomp.

'BURRRRRRRP!'

She bounced off towards the next picnic in a shower of crumbs.

'STOP!' Mr Hyde sprinted after her.

'Sorry!' Nora shouted to the stunned picnickers, as they pelted past. Miss Jex swerved off, and disappeared into a clump of trees.

'Spread out,' Mr Hyde puffed. 'We can corner her here . . .'

He dived into the bushes, followed by Barnaby, Alexis, and Karl. Isaac and Nora ran one way. Jake and Woodstock ran the other.

'There!' Jake spotted a path leading into the trees. They dashed down it into a sun-dappled clearing. Jake squinted around, but there was no sign of Miss Jex.

'She's gone,' Woodstock said, frustrated.

Leaves drifted down from a tree nearby. Shading his eyes, Jake squinted up.

'Up there!' He could just see the red-brown shape of Miss Jex climbing up the trunk.

There was a rustle as Nora and Isaac emerged from a bush.

'Where is she?' cried Isaac. Jake pointed up the tree. Everyone stared up at Miss Jex, leaping from branch to branch.

'She's going to the top,' Woodstock said.

Nora clutched her head. 'The branches will be too thin!'

Miss Jex swung onto a very thin branch.

SNAP!

The branch broke.

CHAPTER 13:

SQUIRREL POWER

'NOOOOOOOOO!' Nora screamed.

Miss Jex plummeted earthwards through the upper branches, grabbing desperately— but they were too thin, and snapped instantly. Jake ran forward, arms outstretched . . .

He caught an armful of leaves and twigs, but no Miss Jex. He looked up.

Miss Jex had managed to grab a bigger

branch and was swinging from it, feet pedalling uselessly in the air.

'WHAT'S GOING ON?!'

A dishevelled Mr Hyde exploded out of the bushes with Alexis, Karl, and Barnaby on his heels. Nora, Isaac, Jake, and Woodstock ran over to him.

'Miss Jex—'

'—up that tree—'

'—she's going to fall!'

Mr Hyde ran to the tree. He grabbed a low branch.

'You can do this, Hydey, my boy,' Jake heard him mutter.

He swung up onto one branch, then another, reciting a sort of mantra.

'Only a little tree, nothing to be scared of . . .'

Nora clutched Jake's sleeve. 'He's scared of heights, remember?' she whispered.

'Don't look down, sir!' Barnaby shouted.

'Nothing to be . . . what?' Mr Hyde looked down.

His face went a ghoulish green. He grabbed the trunk and clung to it, shaking.

'Nice one, Barnaby,' Jake said, crossly.

Alexis ran to the tree. 'Let me go, sir,' she called.

But Mr Hyde took a deep breath, and inched his way up to another branch.

'Oh, he'll never get there,' Isaac groaned, as Mr Hyde stopped again.

'Eeeeeeeek!'

A terrified squawk from Miss Jex made everyone look up. Way up above Mr Hyde, the branch she was hanging from was beginning to bend over.

Clinging to the trunk, Mr Hyde looked up too. When he saw Miss Jex, his face took on a look of steely determination.

'HANG IN THERE, MISS JEX, I'M COMING FOR YOU!' he bellowed.

With a grunt, he pulled himself up, and began scrambling up the tree. Jake watched, mouth open, as his teacher shimmied up the trunk like an overgrown squirrel. In less than thirty seconds, he had squirrelled up to the branch Miss Jex was hanging from. He began to creep along it towards the dangling Miss Jex.

Jake held his breath.

Nora shut her eyes. 'I can't look . . .'

The branch, not used to such enormous squirrels, bent further and further over . . .

There was a frightened squawk. One of Miss Jex's paws had slipped off the branch and she was swinging wildly, trying to catch hold of it again.

Mr Hyde leaned over and made a grab at

Miss Jex's flailing paw.

Creeeee-e-e-e-e-ak . . .

There was a nasty splintering noise.

CRA-A-ACK!!!

'Aaaaa-ah-ah-ah-aaaaaaah!!!!'

With a Tarzan war cry, Mr Hyde flung himself off the branch, scooped Miss Jex up in his arms, and crashed through leaves to land on a thick branch a few metres below.

Jake breathed out.

'HE SAVED HER!!!!' Nora grabbed a startled Isaac and swung him round, whooping, as Mr Hyde swung down to the ground with Miss Jex clinging to him like a baby monkey.

'Mr Hyde, you're a hero!' Woodstock cried.

'Superhero!' Karl added.

'Super-mega-hero!' Nora said, proudly.

'How did you do it, sir?' Jake asked. 'I mean—you're scared of heights!'

Mr Hyde looked up at the tree, then at the little Creature in his arms, who was looking up at him with bushbaby-like eyes.

'I'm not entirely sure,' he said, thoughtfully.

'Maybe he touched some squirrel poo and turned into a squirrel,' Barnaby said, smirking. Nora scowled at him.

'Don't be horrid. Mr Hyde was just really brave,' she said, crossly.

Isaac coughed. 'Nora's right,' he said. 'In moments of extreme danger, people can gain extraordinary strength. Mothers have even been known to lift cars off their children—' He stopped and sniffed. 'What's that smell?'

At the same moment, Jake saw an orange

glow coming from Miss Jex. He could smell something too—a burning smell, like . . .

Burnt toast? In a flash, he realized.

'Miss Jex is changing! Everyone get down!'

Jake threw himself to the ground and covered his eyes.

FAAAAAAAAAAAAAARRRRRT!

Wheeeeeeee . . . .

POP! POP! POP!

BANG!

Silence.

Jake lifted his head. Mr Hyde was still standing at the foot of the tree. In his arms was Miss Jex, steaming a bit, but back to her normal, teachery self.

She gazed up at Mr Hyde. 'Mr Hyde! You rescued me. Even though you're scared of heights!'

Mr Hyde went crimson and hurriedly put her down.

'It was nothing,' he mumbled.

'No, it was brave,' she said, firmly. 'It was your bravery that changed me back!'

Mr Hyde went even deeper red.

'Miss Jex, you've got it wrong,' he stammered. 'It was my fault that you turned into a . . . a Creature. You see, I have this problem . . .'

'That wasn't your fault,' Miss Jex said, gently. 'I must have inherited it from my mother. You see, she used to change into a Creature too.'

Mr Hyde gaped at Miss Jex. 'Your mother?!'

Miss Jex nodded. 'I always thought one day it might happen to me. It must have been the electric shock from the Van de Graaff generator that set me off. Funny—I've always had a thing about electricity! Excuse me, you seem to have a bird's nest in your hair . . .'

She reached out her hand.

'Let me . . .'

Jake started. He could have sworn he saw sparks fly between the two teachers as Miss Jex's hand touched Mr Hyde's hair! He looked closely at his teacher. His face was definitely glowing . . .

'Not again!' Jake started forward.

Nora pulled him back. 'I don't think he's changing, Jake.'

Jake looked at the two teachers. Miss Jex was glowing too! They looked like a pair of giant human-shaped glow sticks.

'So—why are they glowing, then?'

Nora rolled her eyes and drew a heart shape in the air. Jake's eyes widened.

'Ohhhh—*now* I get it!'

More Creature Teacher books, out now!

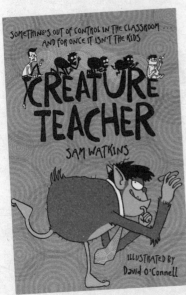

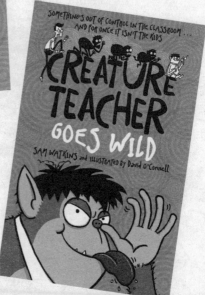

COMING SOON!

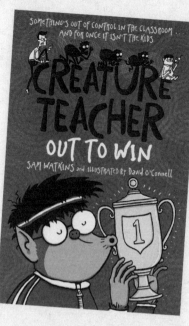

SOMETHING'S OUT OF CONTROL IN THE CLASSROOM... AND FOR ONCE IT ISN'T THE KIDS

CREATURE TEACHER
OUT TO WIN

SAM WATKINS and ILLUSTRATED BY David O'Connell

Creature Teacher Out to Win

Jake and his friends are competing in front of a crowd of thousands at the local football stadium. Well, maybe not thousands, but lots of their mums and dads are there. So when their brilliant teacher, Mr Hyde, turns into a mischievous little creature, how on earth are they going to keep his secret? There's only so long that they can pretend he's the team mascot, and he's certainly not going to play by the rules! It doesn't take long for chaos to kick off when Creature's around!

Turn the page to continue the laughs
with an extract of Creature Teacher!

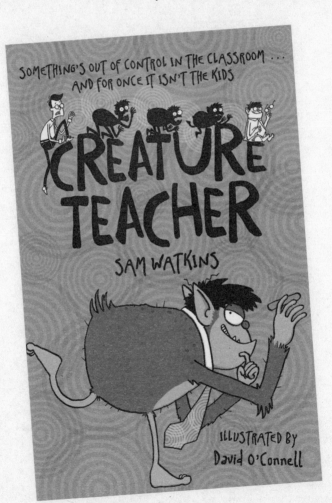

SOMETHING'S OUT OF CONTROL IN THE CLASSROOM . . .
AND FOR ONCE IT ISN'T THE KIDS

CREATURE TEACHER

SAM WATKINS

ILLUSTRATED BY
David O'Connell

RULE 1:

DO NOT GROAN ~~NOT~~ WHEN
ASKED TO RECITE POETRY

(handwritten: LOUDLY inserted above "GROAN WHEN")

B-R-R-R-R-R-R-R-R-R-R-R-R-R-R-
RINNNNNGGGGGGGGGGGGGG-G-G-G!

The school bell screeched in Jake's ear and
he leapt out of the chair with a yelp.

It's a new school, not a shark tank, he told
himself, sitting once more. *But then again—
what if his teacher was an old dragon? What if
he didn't make any friends? What if . . .*

The office door burst open and the secretary bustled out. 'I'll take you to the Head now, dear . . . oops, mind yourself . . . '

Jake found himself being propelled through a stream of noisy pupils that had erupted from nowhere. Minutes later, the corridor was empty again. The secretary stopped outside a door.

On it was a sign that read '**MRS BLUNT**' in large, angry letters. Underneath, in smaller, slightly annoyed letters, it said 'Headteacher'.

'Wait here,' said the secretary. 'The Head will be out shortly.'

A well-disciplined row of chairs stood along the wall and Jake perched on one. A man sat at the other end, his knees nearly grazing his ears. He wore black-rimmed glasses and was tapping a rhythm on his knee.

'MUPPETS!' he exclaimed suddenly.

Jake jumped.

The man chuckled. 'Sorry. I've been trying to work out what that rhythm was and it just struck me—it's the theme from *The Muppet Show*.' He looked at Jake over his glasses.

'Seeing the Head? Are you in trouble?'

'No. It's my first day,' said Jake.

'Ah. I'm a new boy too. Name's Hyde. And you are . . . ?'

'Jake Jones.'

'Delighted to meet you, Jake Jones. Are you nervous?'

Jake lied. 'No.'

'Me neither,' said Mr Hyde. He looked flushed. 'How scary can the Head be, anyway? She won't bite, will she? Heh heh.'

Mr Hyde had gone very red indeed. Even his ears were scarlet. *And—was he actually starting to . . . glow?* Jake wondered.

'If I was nervous,' continued Mr Hyde, 'I'd just tap a rhythm on my knee. Like this.' Mr Hyde drummed his fingers up and down gently on his knee.

Tap-tap-tappity-tap.

Jake rubbed his eyes and looked at Mr Hyde

again. He was a bit pink, but he wasn't glowing.

Suddenly the Headteacher's door burst open and Mr Hyde started tapping his knee furiously.

'MR HYDE! COME IN!' a harsh voice commanded.

Mr Hyde took a deep breath, stood up, and ducked in through the door. It clanged shut.

Jake stared at the closed door. *Had Mr Hyde actually glowed*? He shook his head. He must have imagined it . . . *People don't glow*.

Before Jake had time to think about this, the door opened again. Mr Hyde shuffled out, followed by a dark-haired woman in a suit. She saw Jake, and frowned.

'Oh yes. The new boy. This is your teacher, Mr Hyde. Now, let's get you both to class.'

Mrs Blunt marched them out into a courtyard

with a huge pile of rocks in the middle. She stopped by the rocks, and patted one of them fondly.

'This is my Rockery. All the building work is done by pupils who earn three Sad Faces.

A Sad Face is given for breaking one of the School Rules.'

Jake's eyes met Mr Hyde's. The rocks looked very heavy.

'Our discipline is first-rate,' Mrs Blunt continued, leading them into a corridor, her heels click-clacking on the hard floor. 'I hope you will keep 5b in order, Mr Hyde. They can be . . . lively.'

Jake heard the sound of chatter, getting louder and louder. As they rounded a corner, he saw a gaggle of pupils outside a classroom door. There was pushing, shoving, and loud giggling.

'*Mrs Blunt!*' one of the girls hissed.

The children scurried into line. The hubbub faded. One boy dropped his lunchbox and biscuits rolled across the corridor. He bent to pick them up.

'McCRUMB!' roared Mrs Blunt.

The boy groaned 'Miiiiss . . . ' but got back in line.

'Class 5b. Anyone wishing to work on the Rockery, continue talking. If not, go in, sit down and do not utter a sound.'

The class trooped in. Mrs Blunt stopped the biscuit dropper.

'Barnaby McCrumb. I believe you have two Sad Faces. One more, and I will see you at the Rockery. Understand?'

'Yeeeessss, miss.'

Mrs Blunt glared at Barnaby, but waved him into the silent classroom and marched Jake and Mr Hyde to the front.

'5b, meet Jake Jones, your new classmate,' said Mrs Blunt.

Twenty-five pairs of eyes fixed on Jake. He would rather have been dangling upside down over a tank full of sharks.

'And this is your new teacher, Mr Hyde. To welcome them, I want you to recite my 'Joy of School Rules' poem you've been working on for the Founders' Celebration.'

There was a chorus of groans.

'QUIET! I did *not* give you permission to groan.'

A girl in the front row put her hand up.

'Nora?'

'Miss, we haven't practised for *a-a-a-ages*

because Miss Read said it brought her out in a rash but I thought it might be a tarantula bite because tarantula hairs contain a deadly toxin—'

A boy behind Nora broke in.

'I wrote a tune for it, Miss. Shall I sing it for you?'

'I'm not interested in songs about tarantula hair, Karl. I'm interested in Class 5b reciting my poem at the Founders' Celebration tomorrow: word perfect, with gusto.'

She turned to Mr Hyde.

'The Founders' Evening is an extremely important event, at which all the classes put on a performance to show their appreciation of the ▯ple who established our wonderful school ▯ *excellent* Rules.'

▯inted to a large poster on the back